Chapter 1:

A Chance Encounter at Comic Con

As the doors of the elevator closed, sealing Connor Adams and Fiona Montgomery in together, he couldn't help but feel a slight pang of panic. He had never been a fan of enclosed spaces, and the flickering lights in the malfunctioning elevator didn't help calm his nerves.

Fiona, on the other hand, seemed completely unfazed by the situation. Her colorful wig bobbed as she bounced on the balls of her feet, her slender fingers tapping against a prop sword.

"So," Fiona said, her voice filled with boundless energy, "What brings you to San Diego Comic Con?"

Connor swallowed nervously, trying to come up with a suitable response. "Uh, well, I've always been interested in geek culture, and I thought it would be fun to experience it firsthand."

Fiona's eyes sparkled with excitement. "That's awesome! I've been coming to Comic Con for years, cosplaying as my favorite characters. It's like stepping into a whole new world!"

Connor couldn't help but crack a smile at Fiona's enthusiasm. Despite their differences, there was something infectious about her energy.

"I can see why you love it so much," Connor admitted, his voice wavering slightly.

Fiona grinned, leaning against the elevator wall. "So, tell me, who's your favorite superhero?"

Connor hesitated for a moment, trying to recall the name of a superhero he had heard of recently. "Um... Captain Amazing?"

Fiona burst into laughter, her melodic chuckles filling the confined space. "Oh my god, you mean Captain Apex! That's okay, I forgive you."

Connor's cheeks flushed with embarrassment. "Right, Captain Apex. Sorry about that."

"No worries!" Fiona waved away his apology. "We can catch you up on all the latest superhero news while we explore the convention together."

Table of Contents

AN ORDINARY MAN

ALVARO FIGARES

As the elevator jolted and started moving once again, the pair of them exchanged curious glances.

"Looks like we're back in action," Fiona quipped, resuming her bouncy demeanor.

Connor couldn't help but admire Fiona's ability to find joy in even the most absurd situations. Maybe this convention wouldn't be so bad after all.

The elevator doors finally opened, revealing a bustling sea of cosplayers and enthusiasts. Connor's eyes widened at the sight of the elaborate costumes and vibrant displays.

"Wow," he breathed, his reserved nature momentarily forgotten.

Fiona grinned mischievously. "Ready to dive into the madness?"

Connor took a deep breath, summoning his newfound courage. "Absolutely. Let's do this."

And with that, they plunged headfirst into the chaos and excitement of Comic Con.

They weaved through the crowd, taking in the sights and sounds. Connor found himself laughing at Fiona's comedic attempts to mimic various characters' poses and catchphrases.

"I have to say, this is far more entertaining than I ever imagined it would be," Connor admitted, a genuine smile playing on his lips.

Fiona winked at him, her eyes gleaming with mischief. "Told you it would be a blast."

They continued their exploration of the convention, stumbling upon stalls selling everything from collectibles to homemade costumes.

As they passed by a group of cosplayers dressed as zombies, Connor couldn't resist a playful nudge to Fiona's side.

"You know, I think we make a great team. Like a comic book duo."

Fiona chuckled, bumping him back. "I can picture it now, 'The Awkward Avenger and the Vibrant Vixen.' Our superpower? Awkwardly saving the day."

Connor rolled his eyes with a laugh. "I think our superpower would be turning everyday situations into hilariously absurd ones."

They shared a knowing look, both of them aware that their chance encounter in the elevator had sparked a connection neither of them had expected.

And as they roamed the convention floor, laughter echoed through the halls, a preview of the hilarity and adventures they were about to embark on together.

Chapter 2:
The Unexpected Side Effects of a Costume

The convention floor buzzed with excitement as cosplayers, artists, and fans mingled together in a colorful sea of costumes and merchandise. Connor, feeling slightly overwhelmed, clutched his water bottle tightly, trying to blend in with the bustling crowd. He glanced around, mesmerized by the elaborate cosplays, when suddenly, a clumsy collision sent his drink flying through the air.

SPLASH! The cold liquid drenched a vibrant red and gold costume, causing it to fizzle and spark. "Oh no!" Connor exclaimed, his eyes widening in horror. The cosplayer, Fiona, stared at her malfunctioning outfit with a mix of surprise and dismay. "What happened?" she asked, frantically trying to fix her costume.

"I'm so sorry! It was an accident," Connor stammered, hastily rummaging through his bag for a napkin. "Let me help you." He rushed forward, dabbing at the wet fabric. Little did he know, his unintentional touch of the costume's hidden mechanism would trigger a chain reaction of epic proportions.

Glowing with a blinding light, Fiona's costume suddenly morphed and transformed right before Connor's eyes. The crowd gasped in awe as Fiona stood tall, now adorned in a full-blown superhero outfit, complete with a billowing cape and shiny boots. "What...what just happened?" Connor stuttered, dumbfounded.

Fiona grinned widely, her eyes twinkling with excitement. "I think my costume just gained a mind of its own," she said, testing out her newfound powers with a playful leap into the air. And that's when the chaos began.

People cheered and hollered, drawn by the spectacle of a real-life superhero. Cameras flashed, and a crowd quickly formed around Fiona, eager to capture this unexpected moment. Beaming with pride, she struck a pose, unintentionally causing a gust of wind to blow through the convention hall.

Posters, merchandise, and even unfortunate wigs were sent flying, creating a scene of utter chaos. Vendors scrambled to save their precious goods, while convention-goers either ducked for cover or joined in the uproar. "Fiona, you have to control your powers!" Connor shouted above the commotion, his eyes widening in panic.

"Oops!" Fiona giggled as she accidentally sent a cosplayer's prop soaring into the air. "I guess being a superhero isn't as easy as it looks." She tried to focus, bringing her hands together in a determined manner. "Okay, let me try to rein these powers in."

But despite Fiona's best intentions, her newfound abilities continued to wreak havoc. Lasers, sparks, and gusts of wind shot out in every direction, turning the once lively convention into a battlefield of comical destruction. Connor, overwhelmed, dodged a stray prop and clung onto a nearby booth for dear life.

"I promise, I didn't mean for any of this to happen!" Connor yelped, frantically waving his arms to clear away a cloud of smoke. "We need to get out of here before things get even worse!"

Fiona bit her lip, her eyes searching the chaos for an escape route. "You're right," she conceded, her voice barely audible amidst the mayhem. Grabbing Connor's hand, she led him through the panicked crowd, leaving a comical trail of chaos in their wake.

They stumbled and weaved through the convention hall, narrowly avoiding collisions and flying debris. Connor's heart raced, but he couldn't help but feel a sense of exhilaration amidst the madness. This was turning out to be the most memorable Comic Con ever, even if it meant risking life and limb.

Just as they reached the exit, a voice boomed over the loudspeakers. "Attention, attendees! Please stay calm and evacuate the convention hall. We are addressing the situation and will get everything under control." Startled, Connor glanced at Fiona, his heart sinking. They hadn't caused this mess intentionally, but now they were caught up in the chaos.

Outside, they found a momentary respite as people fumbled their way towards safety. Connor leaned against a wall, gulping in fresh air. "What...what now?" he panted, his hair disheveled and his glasses askew.

Fiona, still radiating with newfound heroism, smiled bravely. "We need to find a way to stop my powers from going haywire. Maybe there's someone here who can help us?"

Just then, a figure approached them, clad in a flowy robe with a long white beard. "Ah, I could not help but overhear your predicament," the man said, his voice wise and melodious. "It seems you require some guidance."

Connor blinked, looking at the man in astonishment. "Are you...a wizard?" he managed to ask, his voice trembling slightly.

The man chuckled warmly, his eyes twinkling with mirth. "Wizard, guru, call me what you like. My name is Dr. Harold Jenkins, and I believe I can help you with Fiona's newfound powers."

Connor's hope reignited like a spark in the darkness. "Please, Dr. Jenkins, we could really use your guidance. Things have gotten completely out of hand."

Nodding sagely, Dr. Jenkins extended a hand towards Fiona. "Give me your other hand, Fiona. Close your eyes and breathe deeply," he instructed, his tone soothing and gentle.

Fiona complied, reaching out and grasping Dr. Jenkins' outstretched hand. Her eyes fluttered closed, and she inhaled deeply, the chaos around them temporarily fading into the background.

Dr. Jenkins began to speak in a low, calming voice. "Fiona, I want you to imagine yourself grounded, connected to the Earth's energy. Feel the power flowing through you, but visualize it as a gentle stream, steady and controlled."

Fiona's body relaxed, the crackling energy dissipating as she envisioned the turbulent waves of power gradually calming. "I... I think I can feel it," she whispered, her voice barely audible.

Connor watched in awe as Fiona's superhero aura dimmed, and the wild powers seemed to stabilize. The crowd, slowly regaining their composure, looked on in anticipation, waiting for the outcome.

With one final deep breath, Fiona opened her eyes, a newfound serenity radiating from within her. "It worked!" she exclaimed, her voice filled with relief. "I think I can control my powers now."

Dr. Jenkins smiled, his eyes crinkling at the corners. "Remember, Fiona, harnessing power is not just about strength, but also about finding balance within yourself. Embrace the absurdity of your situation, and it shall guide you towards resolution."

Fiona nodded, a fierce determination settling in her eyes. "Thank you, Dr. Jenkins. You've given us hope amidst the chaos."

Just then, a booming voice echoed from behind them. "Hold it right there!" Connor and Fiona turned to see Detective Samuel Rodriguez, his gaze fixed on them with suspicion. "What are you two doing here amidst all this chaos?"

Chapter 3:
The Mysterious Meditation Guru

Connor glanced at his watch as he hurried into the meditation seminar. He had barely made it in time, his heart still racing from the excitement of the previous day's events at Comic Con. Little did he know that this seminar would lead him on an unexpected journey of self-discovery.

As he entered the dimly lit room, he saw Dr. Harold Jenkins, a bald man with a long white beard, sitting at the front, surrounded by an air of mystical energy. Connor found a seat towards the back and tried to clear his mind, eager to learn the secrets of meditation.

Just as Dr. Jenkins started speaking, Connor's mind began to wander. He couldn't help but think about the absurd situations he had found himself in, whether it was being trapped in an elevator or witnessing Fiona's newfound superpowers. He wondered how these bizarre occurrences were connected to the universe's cosmic energy.

"Focus on your breath," Dr. Jenkins said, his voice calm and soothing. "Inhale... exhale... let your worries drift away."

Connor took a deep breath, attempting to follow Dr. Jenkins' instructions. But his mind was still full of questions and doubts.

"Excuse me, Dr. Jenkins," Connor raised his hand. "I can't help but wonder... what's the connection between meditation and the absurd situations I've found myself in?"

Dr. Jenkins chuckled softly, his eyes twinkling with humor. "Ah, young one, the mysteries of the universe are not always meant to be understood. Sometimes, it's about embracing the absurdity and finding joy in the chaos."

Connor frowned. "But how can I find joy in chaos? It's not exactly a comfortable situation."

"Comfort is not the goal, my dear boy," Dr. Jenkins replied, his voice wise and gentle. "It's about letting go of control, surrendering to the flow of the universe. Sometimes, the best things in life come from unexpected twists and turns."

Suddenly, the room began to shake, books falling off the shelves and participants gasping in surprise. Connor looked at Dr. Jenkins, his eyes wide with alarm.

"Is this another absurd situation?" Connor asked, his voice tinged with panic.

Dr. Jenkins let out a deep laugh, his laughter echoing through the room. "Ah, my young friend, you have much to learn. The shaking of the room is merely the universe's way of reminding us to embrace the chaos."

Connor blinked in confusion. "So... we're supposed to be joyful about the shaking room?"

"Precisely!" Dr. Jenkins exclaimed, standing up and swaying with the movement of the room. "Life is a grand dance, my boy. And sometimes, the dance floor may be a little shaky."

Connor couldn't help but smile at Dr. Jenkins' infectious enthusiasm. Maybe there was something to this embracing-the-chaos idea after all.

As the shaking subsided, Dr. Jenkins sat back down, his voice reverting to its serene tone. "Now, let us continue our meditation. Close your eyes and imagine yourself floating amidst the cosmic energy of the universe."

Connor closed his eyes and did his best to follow Dr. Jenkins' instructions. He imagined himself floating among the stars, feeling a sense of peace settle over him.

Suddenly, Connor felt a gentle breeze on his skin, like a comforting caress. He opened his eyes and saw Dr. Jenkins standing in front of him, waving his hand in the air.

"How did you...?" Connor asked, his voice filled with awe.

Dr. Jenkins smiled enigmatically. "Ah, my dear boy, the universe works in mysterious ways. Sometimes, it gifts us with little moments of magic to remind us of its infinite possibilities."

Connor couldn't help but chuckle. "Magic, huh? I never thought I'd see the day when I'd learn about cosmic energy and magic tricks in the same breath."

Dr. Jenkins laughed heartily, his eyes sparkling with mischief. "There's more to this world than meets the eye, my young friend. And sometimes, it takes a bit of magic to truly see."

As the meditation seminar drew to a close, Connor felt a newfound sense of peace and acceptance. He realized that life was full of absurd situations, and the best he could do was embrace them and find the humor in the chaos.

Dr. Jenkins approached Connor and placed a hand on his shoulder. "Remember, my boy, the universe has chosen you for a reason. Embrace the absurdity, and you will find your inner strength."

Connor nodded, grateful for Dr. Jenkins' guidance. "Thank you, Dr. Jenkins. I feel like I've learned more about myself in this short time than I have in years."

Dr. Jenkins smiled warmly. "That is the power of embracing the absurd, my boy. It opens doors within ourselves that we never knew existed."

As Connor left the meditation seminar, he couldn't help but hum a tune under his breath. The absurdity of life had become a little less daunting, and he felt a renewed sense of purpose.

Just then, his phone buzzed with a message from Fiona. It seemed that the universe had another adventure in store for them. Connor smiled and hurried off, eager to embrace the next absurd chapter of his life.

Little did he know that this chance encounter with Dr. Jenkins would be the catalyst for even more hilariously unexpected situations. The absurdity of life was just beginning to unfold.

And so, armed with newfound wisdom and a humorous outlook, Connor set off on his next alventure, ready to navigate the chaos with a smile on his face and a mischievous twinkle in his eyes.

Chapter 4:
The Private Investigator's Intriguing Offer

Connor glanced around the dimly lit alley, hoping that his incredulous expression would somehow ward off the absurdity that seemed to follow him wherever he went. Unfortunately, his incredulity had yet to develop such mystical properties. "You've got to be kidding me," he muttered under his breath.

Just as he turned to leave, a sharp and sarcastic voice rang out from behind him. "Well, well, well, if it isn't Mr. Magnet for Mayhem himself. You seem to have a knack for stumbling into the most peculiar situations, don't you?"

Connor turned to face the source of the voice and found himself staring into the piercing gaze of Penny Parker, a private investigator with an energy that matched her vibrant red hair. "Are you following me now?" he asked, a mixture of surprise and annoyance evident in his voice.

Penny smirked, her eyes twinkling with mischief. "No, no, I assure you. It's just a delightful coincidence that we happen to keep bumping into each other during these rather unique occurrences. It seems you have a flair for the absurd, my dear Mr. Adams."

Connor raised an eyebrow, his skepticism plain on his face. "Flair for the absurd, huh? Is that what they're calling it now?"

Penny chuckled, the sound like a delightful melody in a chaotic symphony. "Oh, come now, Connor. You must admit that there's a certain charm to the way you stumble your way through these situations. It takes a special kind of wit and resourcefulness."

Despite his reservations, Connor couldn't help but be intrigued by Penny's words. "Okay, let's say I entertain the thought of investigating these bizarre occurrences. What's in it for you?"

Penny's eyes gleamed with mischief as she leaned closer, her voice dropping to a conspiratorial whisper. "Oh, Connor, my dear, don't you know? Uncovering secrets and exposing hidden truths is my ultimate passion. And you, my friend, seem to be entangled in a web of mysterious conspiracies."

Connor's curiosity got the better of him, and he found himself nodding. "Alright, Parker, you've piqued my interest. Let's dive headfirst into this absurdity together and see what we uncover."

With a grin that held equal parts excitement and determination, Penny extended a hand towards Connor. "Deal."

As they shook hands, a gust of wind whipped through the alley, tossing newspapers and discarded fast food wrappers into the air around them. Connor couldn't help but laugh at the absurdity of the moment.

"Already embracing the chaos, I see," Penny quipped, her voice carrying a note of approval.

Connor chuckled, feeling a newfound sense of camaraderie with Penny. "If life is going to be a series of absurd situations, we might as well dive in headfirst and embrace the madness."

The two of them set off on their investigation, their steps infused with a determination to unravel the hidden conspiracy that had plagued Connor's life. As they dug deeper, the web of deceit grew more intricate, leading to even more bizarre and hilarious situations.

Armed with their wit, resourcefulness, and Penny's sharp investigative skills, they navigated through an underground labyrinth of influential figures, secret societies, and a quirky group of conspiracy theorists who had inexplicably decided to join their cause.

With each absurd situation they encountered, Connor and Penny's bond grew stronger, their banter becoming a symphony of sarcastic jabs and snappy comebacks. They were a perfect pair, one with a talent for stumbling into trouble and the other with a knack for getting them out of it.

As they raced against the clock, their adventures took them to extravagant parties, hidden underground chambers, and even an incident involving a runaway ostrich and a surprise Elvis impersonator. It was ridiculous, it was chaotic, and it was the most fun Connor had ever had.

Along the way, Connor couldn't help but notice the spark of passion in Penny's eyes as they uncovered the truth, piece by absurd piece. It was infectious, and he found himself falling deeper into the clutches of her captivating charm.

Their investigation eventually led them to a final confrontation with the mastermind behind the conspiracy, a man who had remained hidden in the shadows, pulling the strings like a deranged puppeteer.

As the truth was finally revealed, the mastermind's sinister deeds laid bare for all to see, Connor couldn't help but feel a sense of satisfaction. "We did it, Penny," he said, his voice filled with both relief and triumph.

Penny nodded, her hand resting gently on Connor's arm. "Yes, we did. And I have to say, of all the absurdities I've encountered, you, Mr. Adams, have proven to be the most delightful."

Connor's heart skipped a beat at her words, and a flush crept onto his cheeks. "I... I don't even know what to say."

Penny grinned, her eyes sparkling with mischief. "You don't have to say anything, my dear. Just keep being your wonderfully absurd self, and I suspect there may be more adventures in our future."

And with a knowing wink, Penny turned on her heels, her red hair swaying with a playful flourish. "Until next time, Connor."

As he watched her disappear into the night, a mix of anticipation and excitement filled Connor's heart. He knew that with Penny by his side, there would always be more absurdities to embrace, and he couldn't wait to dive headfirst into the next adventure.

And so, with a smile on his face and a renewed sense of purpose, Connor set off into the night, ready to face whatever chaos and hilarity the world had in store for him.

After all, life was too short to hold back – might as well dance with the absurd, laugh in the face of chaos, and let the cosmos guide the way.

As Connor walked away from the alley, he couldn't help but hum a tune, his steps light and filled with newfound joy. The world was his stage, and he was ready to play his part to the fullest.

And so, the unlikely duo of Connor and Penny ventured forth, their laughter mingling with the chaos, their hearts open to the unexpected.

The absurdity of life beckoned them, and they were more than ready to answer the call.

Little did they know that their next adventure would take them to the eccentric world of a retired magician, where illusions and tricks would test their wit and resilience. But that, dear reader, is a tale for another chapter.

Chapter 5:
The Eccentric Inventor's Unexpected Gadgets

Connor walked into the cluttered workshop, his eyes widening at the sight before him. It was filled with strange gadgets, flashing lights, and a cacophony of clinks and beeps. Sitting amidst it all was Maxine Collins, an eccentric inventor with wild, unkempt hair and a mischievous gleam in her eyes.

"Welcome to my humble abode!" Max exclaimed, giving Connor a mischievous grin. "I see you're finally ready to embrace the madness and join our little team!"

Connor looked around, still trying to process the chaotic workshop. "I must admit, Max, this is... quite something. What exactly do you invent here?"

Max laughed, a mischievous twinkle in her eyes. "Oh, my dear Connor, I invent the unconventional, the unexpected, and the downright absurd! My creations are equal parts ingenious and unpredictable."

Intrigued, Connor approached a table covered in a multitude of buttons, levers, and gears. "Can you give me an example?"

Max grinned, her eyes sparkling. "Why, of course!" She picked up a small device that looked like a hybrid of a flashlight and a harmonica. "Behold, the Sonic Harmonizer! This little beauty emits sonic frequencies that can disrupt electronics within a ten-meter radius."

Connor blinked, his interest piqued. "That sounds... incredibly useful."

Max shrugged, a mischievous gleam in her eyes. "Depends on the situation, my friend. Sometimes, you need to disable those pesky security cameras to make a dramatic entrance, or perhaps you just want to annoy your neighbors with some well-timed harmonica blasts."

Connor laughed, unable to resist the infectious energy radiating from Max. "I can see how that could come in handy. What else do you have?"

Max's smile widened as she held up what appeared to be an ordinary pen. "Ah, the Pen of Truth! With a press of this button, it reveals the true intentions of anyone you point it at. Perfect for cutting through the bull."

Connor raised an eyebrow, both amused and intrigued. "And what if someone has nothing to hide?"

Max shrugged, a mischievous grin on her face. "Oh, don't worry, I'm sure we can find something juicy to reveal. Everyone's got secrets!"

As the laughter subsided, Max's expression turned serious. "But in all seriousness, Connor, my inventions may be odd, but they serve a purpose. We're going to need them as we delve deeper into this conspiracy."

Connor nodded, feeling a sense of reassurance in Max's words. "I trust your creativity and resourcefulness, Max. I have a feeling your inventions will prove vital on our journey."

Max smirked, her excitement palpable. "That's what I like to hear, Connor! Embrace the chaos, my friend, and together, we'll uncover the truth!"

As the group prepared to embark on their next adventure, Connor couldn't help but feel a sense of anticipation. The combination of Max's eccentric inventions, Penny's sharp wit, and his own newfound resilience filled him with a sense of hope.

They stepped out into the night, their footsteps echoing through the quiet streets. Connor couldn't resist a chuckle as he glanced at Max. "So, Max, any gadgets up your sleeve for this particular mission?"

Max grinned mischievously, her eyes glinting with anticipation. "Oh, you have no idea, Connor. I've crafted a device that can transform you into a miniature squirrel for those hard-to-reach places. Trust me, it'll be nuts!"

Connor burst into laughter, the absurdity of the situation sinking in. "A miniature squirrel? Max, you really do have a solution for everything."

Max winked, her excitement contagious. "That's what I'm here for, Connor. To add a little sparkle of absurdity to the chaos."

As they made their way through the darkened streets, Connor couldn't help but feel a surge of gratitude for the unique individuals he had met on his journey. Each one brought something extraordinary to the table, their quirks blending seamlessly to create a vibrant tapestry of laughter, camaraderie, and inventive chaos.

Suddenly, an ear-piercing screech cut through the night air, sending shivers down Connor's spine. He turned to Max, his eyes wide with concern.

Max's eyes glinted with mischief. "Don't worry, Connor. That was just my Sonic Harmonizer kicking into action. We've got company!"

Connor's heart raced as the chaos of their situation intensified. The group huddled together, each member reaching for their own absurd gadgets, ready to face whatever challenges lay ahead.

As they rounded the corner, they found themselves face-to-face with a group of mysterious figures, eyes glowing in the moonlight. Their presence sent a chill down Connor's spine, but he refused to let fear overtake him. With Max and her unconventional inventions at his side, they were ready to face any obstacle.

"Alright, Max, showtime," Connor muttered, his voice laden with determination.

Max nodded, her eyes fixed on the figures before them. "Get ready, Connor. I've got just the gadget for this. Brace yourself!"

Max held up a small device that resembled a giant rubber band. "Presenting the Distracto-Bouncer! Launch it in the air, and it'll bounce around, emitting dazzling lights and confusing noises. It'll give us the perfect distraction to make our move."

Connor couldn't help but grin, feeling a surge of anticipation. "Now that's what I call an entrance!"

With a flick of Max's wrist, the Distracto-Bouncer soared through the air, ricocheting off walls and floors, filling the space with dazzling lights and cacophonous noises. As confusion engulfed their mysterious adversaries, Connor and his team seized the opportunity to spring into action.

27

Chapter 6:
Detective Rodriguez's Suspicious Pursuit

Detective Samuel Rodriguez sat in his dimly lit office, poring over the case files spread out on his desk. His sharp eyes narrowed as he sifted through the evidence, connecting the dots in his mind. He had a hunch, a feeling that Connor Adams was more than just an innocent bystander caught in a web of absurd situations.

Feeling a mounting frustration, Detective Rodriguez closed the file and leaned back in his chair. He couldn't shake the suspicion that there was something more to Connor's involvement, something hiding beneath the surface. It was his job to uncover the truth.

With a determined expression, Detective Rodriguez reached for his cell phone and dialed a number he had memorized. As he listened to the dial tone, he couldn't help but wonder why he felt such an intense need to pursue Connor relentlessly.

"Hello?" a voice answered on the other end of the line. It was a raspy voice, filled with intrigue and mystery. "Detective Rodriguez, how can I be of service?"

"Mr. Johnson," Detective Rodriguez spoke, his voice low and serious. "I need your expertise on a certain individual. His name is Connor Adams."

"Ah, a man surrounded by chaos and absurdity," Henry Johnson replied, a hint of amusement in his tone. "What can you tell me about him, Detective?"

Detective Rodriguez cleared his throat, trying to put his thoughts into words. "Connor Adams seems to be at the center of bizarre events and conspiracies. There's a pattern, Mr. Johnson, and I intend to uncover it."

"A pattern, you say?" Henry Johnson hummed playfully. "Tell me, Detective, what is your gut feeling about Mr. Adams?"

"My gut feeling? It's a mix of suspicion and fascination," Detective Rodriguez admitted, his voice betraying a hint of curiosity that he couldn't suppress. "There's something about him that draws me in, something that doesn't add up."

Henry chuckled softly on the other end of the line. "Detective, my friend, you've stumbled upon something intriguing indeed. The universe has its way of weaving the most absurd tales, and sometimes, the truth lies in the most unexpected places."

"Are you suggesting there's some cosmic force at play here?" Detective Rodriguez asked skeptically.

"In a way, yes," Henry replied cryptically. "But you must tread carefully, Detective. The line between logic and chaos is thin, and it's easy to get lost in the absurdity of it all."

Detective Rodriguez furrowed his brow. "Are you saying I should back off? Drop the case?"

"Not at all, my friend," Henry reassured him. "Embrace the chaos, but do so with caution. The answers you seek may lie beyond what you consider normal or rational."

Detective Rodriguez pondered Henry's words for a moment, weighing his options. The desire to uncover the truth fought against the warnings of embracing the chaos.

With a determined smirk, he made up his mind. "No, Mr. Johnson. I won't back down. I'll follow this trail of absurdity until I uncover the truth, no matter where it leads."

Henry's chuckle resonated through the phone. "I knew you'd say that, Detective. Embrace the absurdity. Embrace the unexpected. That's where the truth lies."

With newfound resolve, Detective Rodriguez hung up the phone and prepared to dive deeper into the investigation. He wouldn't let Connor Adams slip through his fingers. He had personal motives and he would prove it, one absurd clue at a time.

The detective's pursuit of Connor intensified, leading to a game of cat and mouse. Connor felt the weight of suspicion growing stronger, the detective always one step behind. It seemed Detective Rodriguez was determined to expose Connor's secrets, no matter the cost.

The tension between them reached new heights as Connor struggled to maintain his composure and keep his team safe. He had to outsmart the detective, to uncover the truth of the conspiracy while staying one step ahead.

Connor's mind became a whirlwind of strategies, as he, Penny, and Max devised intricate plans to throw Detective Rodriguez off their trail. It was a battle of wits, with absurd misdirections and elaborate ruses employed to keep the detective guessing.

Through clever disguises, quick thinking, and a touch of luck, Connor and his team managed to stay ahead of Detective Rodriguez. The detective's frustration grew, fueling his determination to expose Connor's secrets.

Late one night, as Connor lay in bed, his mind racing with thoughts of the detective, he received an anonymous email. It contained cryptic clues and a meeting place. It was an opportunity to delve deeper into the conspiracy.

With a mix of trepidation and excitement, Connor met the mysterious informant, hoping to gain insight into Detective Rodriguez's motives. What he discovered was shocking and only deepened the mystery surrounding his own involvement.

"It appears, Mr. Adams, that Detective Samuel Rodriguez has a personal vendetta against you," the informant revealed, their voice laced with a mix of fear and secrecy. "He blames you for something in the past, something he's been nursing like a festering wound."

Connor's heart pounded in his chest as he absorbed the revelation. The personal motives of Detective Rodriguez added a twisted layer to their already tumultuous relationship. Connor vowed to uncover the truth behind the detective's vendetta, no matter what it took.

Armed with new information and a sense of urgency, Connor shared the details with Penny and Max. They huddled together, formulating a plan to confront Detective Rodriguez and confront his personal grudge.

The stage was set for a showdown, a clash of absurdity and determination. Connor, Penny, and Max would face the detective head-on, unveiling his true intentions and unraveling the twisted web he had spun.

As they approached Detective Rodriguez's office building, Connor couldn't help but feel a mix of apprehension and determination. The moment of truth was upon them, and the battle of wits would finally come to a head.

With a deep breath, Connor approached the detective's office door, ready to confront the man who tormented him with suspicion and unwavering pursuit. The game was far from over, and in the midst of chaos and absurdity, Connor would face his greatest challenge yet.

The chapter ends with Connor reaching out to open the detective's office door, tension swirling in the air.

Chapter 7:
The Supernatural Connection

Connor stood outside a dimly lit bookstore, his curiosity piqued by the sign that read "Paranormal Investigations." He pushed open the creaky door and stepped inside, greeted by shelves lined with dusty books on ghosts, witches, and otherworldly creatures.

A woman with long, flowing black hair stood behind the counter, flipping through a worn-out journal. She looked up as the bell above the door jingled, her piercing blue eyes meeting Connor's. "Can I help you?" she asked, a hint of intrigue in her voice.

Connor approached the counter, his brows furrowing. "I heard you might be able to shed some light on the...absurd situations in my life," he said cautiously.

The woman's lips curled into a mysterious smile. "Ah, you must be Connor Adams," she said, her voice laced with an ethereal quality. "I've been expecting you. I am Cassandra Miller, but you can call me Cassie."

Connor's eyes widened in surprise. "You know who I am?" he asked, taken aback by her familiarity.

Cassie nodded, her gaze fixed on him. "The supernatural has a way of weaving threads, connecting seemingly unrelated tales," she explained. "And your story, Connor Adams, is intertwined with forces beyond comprehension."

Intrigued, Connor leaned in closer. "What do you mean by 'forces beyond comprehension'?" he asked, his voice filled with both curiosity and trepidation.

Cassie's eyes sparkled with a glint of excitement. "You see, Connor, the absurd situations you find yourself in are not mere coincidence," she began. "There is a supernatural energy at play, guiding you through a series of trials and revelations."

Connor's mind whirled with questions. "So, you're saying there's some kind of hidden meaning behind all of this?" he asked, his voice tinged with a mix of hope and skepticism.

Cassie nodded. "Indeed, Connor. The universe has chosen you for a purpose, and it is my role to help you unravel the mysteries that lie within. The absurdity of your life is but a mask for the supernatural connections that bind us all."

A flicker of unease crossed Connor's face. "But what does all of this mean for me? What am I supposed to do with this knowledge?" he asked, his voice tinged with a hint of uncertainty.

Cassie's expression softened, her voice calm and reassuring. "Embrace it, Connor. Embrace the absurdity, the chaos, and the unknown. Only by accepting the supernatural connections can you uncover the truth and fulfill your destiny."

Connor took a deep breath, his mind racing with the weight of the possibilities laid before him. "Alright, Cassie. I'm in. I'll embrace the absurdity and delve into this supernatural world. But I'll need your guidance," he said determinedly.

Cassie smiled knowingly, her eyes shining with wisdom. "We shall embark on this mystical journey together, Connor. Follow me, and let us unveil the secrets hidden in the shadows."

Connor followed Cassie through the dimly lit bookstore, shelves of forgotten knowledge standing as silent witnesses to their quest. They arrived at a hidden chamber adorned with ancient symbols and mysterious artifacts, a place teeming with the energy of the supernatural.

Cassie motioned for Connor to take a seat on a worn-out leather chair. "Prepare yourself, Connor. We are about to delve into the depths of the supernatural realms," she said, her voice filled with anticipation.

Connor sat down, his heart pounding with a mix of excitement and trepidation. "I'm ready," he said, his voice firm and resolute.

Cassie closed her eyes, her hands hovering over a crystal ball placed on a nearby pedestal. "Focus your thoughts, Connor. Reach out to the hidden corners of your mind. Let the supernatural guide you."

As Connor concentrated, a soft glow enveloped the room, dancing shadows casting strange shapes on the walls. He could feel a presence, an otherworldly force that seemed to beckon him.

Suddenly, the crystal ball lit up, swirling with a mesmerizing array of colors. Images flashed before Connor's eyes, snippets of his past, present, and future intertwining in a mesmerizing dance.

Cassie's voice broke through the trance. "Embrace the connection, Connor. The supernatural is your ally, your guide. Allow it to show you the path."

Connor felt a surge of exhilaration and confidence. His mind cleared, and a newfound clarity washed over him. He knew now that he had to confront the enigmatic forces pulling his strings.

With a determined glint in his eyes, Connor rose from the chair, ready to face whatever challenges lay ahead. "Thank you, Cassie. I will embrace the supernatural connection and follow it to the answers I seek," he declared.

Cassie's smile widened, a knowing glimmer in her eyes. "You have the spark within you, Connor. Embrace the absurdity, and the supernatural will guide you towards the truth."

As Connor stepped out of the hidden chamber, his mind buzzed with a renewed energy. He now possessed a supernatural compass, a connection to the unknown that would lead him to unravel the secrets of his own existence.

The convergence of the supernatural and the absurdity of his life no longer seemed overwhelming but rather an intricate tapestry waiting to be deciphered.

Connor turned back to Cassie, his gratitude evident in his voice. "Thank you, Cassie. You've given me a new purpose and a thrilling journey ahead. Together, we shall unravel the mysteries that bind us."

Cassie nodded, her eyes filled with a mixture of pride and excitement. "Indeed, Connor. Together, we shall navigate the realms of the supernatural and discover the truths that lie within. The path ahead may be filled with chaos and absurdity, but fear not, for the supernatural will illuminate the way."

With newfound determination, Connor set off into the night, his heart full of anticipation and wonder. He was ready to embrace the supernatural connection and embark on a journey that would defy logic and challenge the boundaries of his imagination.

As the door of the paranormal bookstore closed behind him, a gust of wind whispered through the streets, carrying with it a whispered promise of extraordinary adventures to come.

Chapter 8:
Unmasking the Unknown Enemy

Richie Thompson, a charismatic stand-up comedian with a mischievous smile and a twisted sense of humor, emerged from the shadows, making his way towards Connor. "Well, well, well, if it isn't Connor Adams," Richie drawled, his voice dripping with mocking delight.

Connor eyed him warily, his heart pounding in his chest. He had heard stories of Richie's notorious pranks and ruthless sense of humor. "What do you want, Richie?" Connor asked, trying to maintain his composure.

Richie's mischievous smile widened into a wicked grin. "Oh, nothing much, just a little payback for all the times you've stolen the spotlight from me," he replied, his tone laced with venom.

"I've never stolen any spotlight from you," Connor retorted, his voice filled with confusion. "I'm just an ordinary office worker. Why would you target me?"

Richie chuckled darkly, his eyes glinting with malice. "Oh, Connor, my dear old pal, you underestimate the power of jealousy. You may be ordinary, but the absurd situations you find yourself in, the way everything falls into place for you... it's infuriating."

Penny and Max exchanged a glance, realizing that Richie's vendetta against Connor ran deeper than they had anticipated.

"So, you've been orchestrating all of these absurd situations just to get back at me?" Connor asked incredulously.

Richie shrugged nonchalantly, a mischievous glint in his eyes. "Wouldn't you do the same in my position, Connor? I couldn't let you have all the laughs, now could I? It's time someone put you in your place."

Connor's mind raced, trying to come up with a plan to outsmart Richie and reveal his true intentions to the world. He couldn't let Richie continue manipulating others and sabotaging his life.

"Well, Richie, I hate to be the bearer of bad news, but you're not as clever as you think you are. My team and I will uncover your motivations and put an end to your little game," Connor declared, his voice filled with determination.

Richie laughed, a sinister sound that echoed through the room. "Oh, I'm looking forward to that, Connor. Let's see who comes out on top. May the best man win," he taunted, his eyes gleaming with excitement.

As Richie turned to leave, Connor couldn't help but notice the glint of a hidden camera in his jacket pocket. A wave of realization washed over him. Richie had been recording their conversation, planning to use it against him later.

"Hey, Richie! Before you go," Connor called out, a mischievous smirk tugging at the corners of his lips.

Richie turned back, eyebrow raised in curiosity. "What is it, Connor? Have you finally come to your senses and realized that you're no match for me?"

Connor chuckled, shaking his head. "On the contrary, Richie. I just want to make a little wager. You see, I believe in the power of truth, and I'm willing to bet that when the truth comes out, you'll be the one left stunned."

Richie's eyes narrowed, suspicion flickering across his face. "What kind of wager are we talking about, Connor?"

Connor grinned, knowing that he had struck a nerve. "If the truth reveals that you orchestrated all of this, confess and publicly apologize. But if it turns out that I'm wrong, I'll publicly admit that you've bested me."

Richie hesitated for a moment, his mind whirling with thoughts. Finally, a sinister smile spread across his face. "You're on, Connor. Let's see who's laughing when the truth comes out."

With that, Richie sauntered out of the room, leaving Connor and his team to devise a plan to expose him and reveal his deceptive tactics.

"We can't let Richie get away with this," Penny said, her eyes burning with determination. "We need to gather evidence, expose his true intentions, and show the world who he really is."

Max nodded in agreement. "You're right, Penny. It's time to put our wits to the test and outsmart Richie at his own game. We'll have the last laugh."

Connor felt a surge of adrenaline coursing through his veins. He knew their battle against Richie would be filled with absurdity and tension, but he was ready to face it head-on. "Let the showdown begin," he declared.

Over the next few days, Connor and his team tirelessly gathered evidence, analyzed Richie's past behavior, and planned their moves with precision.

They dug deep into Richie's past, unraveling a web of deceit and manipulation that left them astounded. Richie had a history of playing with people's lives, using his comedic talents to mask his true intentions.

As their investigation progressed, they found allies in unexpected places. Fellow comedians, who had fallen victim to Richie's schemes, offered their support and shared their stories, adding strength to the mounting case against him.

Finally, the day of reckoning arrived. Connor, Penny, Max, and their newfound allies gathered in a packed auditorium, ready to expose Richie's true colors.

Connor took a deep breath, his heart pounding in his chest. He stepped onto the stage, facing a sea of expectant faces.

"Ladies and gentlemen, thank you for joining us today," Connor began, his voice filled with purpose. "We are here to unveil the truth, to unmask the unknown enemy who has been manipulating us for far too long."

The room fell silent, the air thick with anticipation. Connor took a moment to let the tension build, relishing in the absurdity of the situation.

"Richie Thompson," Connor declared, his voice ringing with authority. "Your time of laughter and manipulation ends here. It's time to reveal the true face behind that mischievous smile."

Chapter 9:
The Friend Turned Foe

As Connor walked into his favorite yoga studio, he felt a sudden chill in the air. Something was off, and he couldn't quite put his finger on it. Olivia, his yoga instructor and close friend, was standing at the front, her usually warm smile replaced by a cold, calculating gaze.

"Good morning, everyone," Olivia said, her voice dripping with venom. "Today, we'll be focusing on the warrior poses. Let's see if you can handle it."

Connor exchanged puzzled looks with the other yoga participants, unsure of what had caused Olivia's sudden change in demeanor. Nevertheless, he decided to play along and positioned himself at the back of the class.

As they started the first warrior pose, Connor couldn't help but notice how Olivia's movements seemed more forceful and aggressive than usual. She was pushing everyone to their limits, double the intensity they were used to.

"Olivia, what's going on?" Connor whispered, hoping to get an explanation for her behavior. But she simply ignored him, focusing solely on the yoga moves.

As the class progressed, Olivia's aggression only intensified. She seemed hell-bent on making Connor suffer through the most challenging poses.

"Feel the burn! Embrace the struggle!" Olivia shouted, a sinister glint in her eyes. "You thought you could get away with it, didn't you, Connor?"

Connor's heart raced as he struggled to keep up with the demanding poses. He desperately tried to understand what he had done to upset Olivia, but his mind drew a blank.

"Olivia, please!" Connor pleaded. "If I did something wrong, just tell me!"

Olivia didn't respond, her silence causing more confusion and frustration to brew within Connor. He fought through the pain, determined to uncover the truth.

After what felt like an eternity, the yoga class finally came to an end. Olivia dismissed everyone but turned her attention solely to Connor.

"It's time to face the consequences of your actions, Connor," Olivia growled, her voice sending shivers down his spine. "I won't rest until you've suffered as much as I have."

Connor's mind raced, desperately trying to recall any incident that could have caused Olivia such anguish. But nothing came to mind. Perhaps he had inadvertently hurt her without realizing it.

"Olivia, I'm so sorry if I've done something to upset you," Connor said, his voice filled with genuine concern. "Please, tell me what happened."

Olivia's lips curled into a cold smile, her eyes gleaming with satisfaction. "Oh, Connor, you really think an apology will fix everything? You've underestimated me."

Confusion turned into panic as Connor realized Olivia's plan involved more than just physical exertion. There was something much more sinister at play.

Just as Connor prepared to defend himself, Penny and Max burst into the studio, sensing the danger that loomed over him.

"What's going on here?" Penny demanded, her eyes narrowing at Olivia. "If you think you can intimidate Connor, you've got another thing coming."

Olivia scoffed, her gaze flickering between Connor and his newfound allies. "You think you can protect him? You're all in for a rude awakening."

With that, Olivia launched herself at Connor, her lithe frame suddenly filled with the strength of a raging bull. Connor barely managed to dodge her attack, his heart pounding in his chest.

"Olivia, please stop!" Connor pleaded, his voice laced with desperation. "We can talk about this, find a way to resolve whatever issue you have against me."

Instead of responding, Olivia charged at Connor again, her eyes blazing with fury. Connor, fueled by adrenaline, dodged her attack once more, only narrowly avoiding her deadly strikes.

"This isn't you, Olivia!" Max shouted, throwing a cleverly crafted gadget at her feet. Smoke billowed out, temporarily obscuring Olivia's vision.

"Ha! You think some flashy gadgets will stop me?" Olivia's voice floated out of the smoke, tinged with a mixture of arrogance and hatred.

As the smoke cleared, Olivia had disappeared, leaving the three friends to wonder where she had gone. They exchanged worried glances, silently agreeing that Olivia was more dangerous than they had ever anticipated.

"We can't let her get away," Penny said, determination burning in her eyes. "She's a threat to all of us."

Connor nodded, his mind already racing with plans to uncover Olivia's motives and bring an end to her relentless pursuit. "We need to stay one step ahead of her. Let's gather all the information we can."

"Agreed," Max chimed in. "I have a few gadgets that might come in handy. We can use them to track Olivia and uncover her next move."

The three friends formed a circle, their hands joining in a show of solidarity. They may have been caught off guard by Olivia's betrayal, but they were not about to let her tear them apart.

With renewed determination, they set off on their mission, ready to uncover Olivia's motives and protect themselves from her vengeful vendetta.

Chapter 10:
Embracing the Unexpected with a Retired Magician

Connor walked into a dimly lit room, filled with the aroma of old books and mystery. He had been told that this was the place he would meet Henry Johnson, the retired magician who was said to have a knack for finding humor in even the most chaotic situations.

As Connor's eyes adjusted to the low light, he saw a figure sitting at a table covered in playing cards, top hats, and various magical props. It was Henry Johnson, dressed in a sharp suit with a mischievous twinkle in his eye.

"Ah, so you must be Connor," Henry said, giving Connor a once-over. "I've heard quite a bit about you and your adventures. Sit, sit! Let's see if we can work some magic together."

Connor took a seat across from Henry, feeling a mixture of excitement and trepidation. "I've been told that you have a unique perspective on life's absurdities. I could use a little magic in my own chaotic journey."

Henry grinned and picked up a deck of cards, shuffling them skillfully between his fingers. "Magic, my boy, is not just about pulling rabbits out of hats or making things disappear. It's about finding joy in the unexpected, embracing the chaos, and using it to your advantage."

"But how do I find humor in the midst of all the madness?" Connor asked, his brow furrowing in confusion.

Henry chuckled and placed a card in front of Connor. "Life is nothing if not a series of tricks and illusions. Just like this card," he said, pointing to it. "It may seem ordinary, but with a flick of the wrist, it becomes something extraordinary. Embrace the unexpected, my boy, and let the magic unfold."

As Henry spoke, he performed a simple trick, making the card levitate in mid-air. Connor's eyes widened in amazement, and a smile crept onto his face.

"You see, Connor, life is full of surprises. Sometimes, we find ourselves in situations that seem impossible or absurd. But that's where the real magic happens. In those moments, we have the opportunity to create something extraordinary."

Connor nodded, starting to understand. "So, instead of being overwhelmed by the chaos, I should find a way to use it to my advantage?"

Henry nodded approvingly. "Exactly. Embrace the unexpected, find the humor in the absurd, and let it be your guide. That's when the real magic happens."

With Henry's guidance, Connor began to see the world through a new lens. They practiced tricks together, with Henry teaching Connor the art of misdirection and sleight of hand.

As they spent more time together, Connor learned to navigate through the absurd situations with grace and wit. He would chuckle as he found himself jumping over banana peels or maneuvering around random gnomes that seemed to pop up out of nowhere.

Henry's enigmatic nature added a touch of magic to their adventures. He would pull rabbits out of hats or make flowers bloom from thin air, always with a mischievous smile on his face.

In one particularly memorable moment, Connor and Henry found themselves trapped in a room with dozens of doors, each leading to a different chaotic situation. Instead of panicking, Henry simply twirled his wand and said, "Let's see where these rabbit holes take us, my boy."

They stepped through door after door, facing absurd challenges and surprises at every turn. There were talking teapots, gravity-defying staircases, and even a room filled with flying unicorns.

"I thought you said magic wasn't just about pulling rabbits out of hats," Connor exclaimed, laughing as they narrowly avoided being trampled by a stampede of miniature ponies.

Henry winked. "True, my boy, but sometimes, a little bit of classic magic is just what the situation calls for."

As they emerged from the final door, both covered in snowflakes and unicorn glitter, they found themselves standing in the middle of a bustling street. Henry raised his wand and sprouted a bouquet of roses, handing one to Connor.

"Remember, my boy, the real magic lies in finding joy amidst the chaos. Embrace the absurdity, and let it guide you to unexpected wonders," Henry said, his voice filled with warmth and wisdom.

Connor took a deep breath, the scent of the roses filling his senses. He looked around at the busy street, the chaos and laughter of the city enveloping him. It was in that moment that he truly understood what Henry meant.

From that day forward, Connor embraced the unexpected with a newfound zest for life. He saw the humor in the most chaotic situations and used it to his advantage, navigating through each adventure with grace and wit.

As they bid their farewells, Henry handed Connor a small top hat. "Remember, my boy, the magic is within you. Embrace your own unique brand of absurdity and let it shine."

With a mischievous smile, Connor placed the top hat on his head. "Thank you, Henry. I'll carry your wisdom and magic with me wherever I go."

Henry tipped his own hat in farewell. "Go forth, my boy, and create your own extraordinary magic."

With those words echoing in his mind, Connor stepped onto the bustling street, ready for the next adventure life had in store. He walked with a spring in his step, the top hat perched on his head, and a twinkle in his eye.

As he passed by a group of pigeons gathered around a pretzel stand, he couldn't help but chuckle. "Ah, the absurdity of it all," he murmured to himself.

Moments later, a pigeon swooped down, grabbed the pretzel, and flew directly into Connor's face. He burst out laughing, attracting puzzled looks from passersby. But Connor didn't care. He had embraced the unexpected, and it had rewarded him with a hilarious and unexpected souvenir.

With a full-hearted laugh, Connor continued on his way, knowing that wherever chaos and absurdity lurked, he would be there, ready to find the magic within it all.

And so, with each new adventure, each unexpected twist and turn, Connor continued to embrace the chaos and find humor in the absurd. As he embarked on his next journey, he couldn't help but laugh, knowing that the magic of the unknown awaited him.

READER'S GUIDE

In order of importance, we list below the main characters involved in this work.

Name: Connor Adams

Age: 35

Job: Office worker

Role: Protagonist

Appearance: Average height, brown hair, glasses, always dressed in business casual attire

Personality: Easily flustered, well-meaning, quick-witted

Background

Connor is an ordinary man living a mundane life in San Diego. He has a routine job and enjoys a quiet existence. However, his life takes a comedic turn when he finds himself in bizarre and absurd situations, often due to his own clumsiness or sheer bad luck.

Name: Fiona Montgomery

Age: 30

Job: Cosplay enthusiast

Role: Love interest

Appearance: Vibrant colored hair, multiple tattoos, always seen in elaborate and detailed costumes

Personality: Free-spirited, adventurous, outgoing

Background

Fiona is a cosplayer who frequents various conventions in San Diego. She has a passion for creating intricate costumes and enjoys immersing herself in the world of fantasy. She meets Connor at a cosplay convention, and their chance encounter leads to a series of comical misadventures.

Name: Dr. Harold Jenkins

    Age: 50

    Job: Meditation guru

    Role: Mentor

    Appearance: Bald, long white beard, wears flowing robes

    Personality: Wise, calm, mystical

    Background

Dr. Jenkins is a renowned meditation guru who unintentionally becomes Connor's mentor. He possesses a wealth of knowledge about the universe and imparts his wisdom to Connor, often in the most unexpected and hilarious ways.

Name: Penelope "Penny" Parker

Age: 25

Job: Private investigator

Role: Sidekick

Appearance: Sleek, athletic build, always wearing a trench coat

Personality: Sharp, resourceful, sarcastic

Background

Penny is a skilled private investigator who crosses paths with Connor during one of his absurd situations. With her expertise and quick thinking, she becomes an indispensable ally to Connor, helping him navigate through the chaos and uncovering hidden truths.

Name: Maxine "Max" Collins

Age: 40

Job: Eccentric inventor

Role: Comic relief

Appearance: Wild, unkempt hair, lab coat, constantly surrounded by strange gadgets

Personality: Sarcastic, intelligent, quirky

Background

Max is an eccentric inventor who serves as the comic relief in Connor's adventures. Her sarcastic humor and unconventional gadgets often provide much-needed levity in tense situations, making her an invaluable member of Connor's team.

Name: Detective Samuel Rodriguez

Age: 45

Job: Police detective

Role: Suspicious character

Appearance: Meticulously groomed, always in a suit

Personality: Sharp, determined, secretive

Background

Detective Rodriguez is a seasoned police detective who is assigned to investigate the strange occurrences surrounding Connor. He seems to always be one step ahead, raising suspicions about his true intentions and involvement in the absurd situations Connor finds himself in.

Name: Cassandra "Cassie" Miller
Age: 28
Job: Paranormal investigator
Role: Parallel subplot
Appearance: Edgy, tattooed, dressed in gothic attire
Personality: Mysterious, intuitive, fascinated by the supernatural
Background
Cassie is a paranormal investigator who becomes entangled in Connor's story when they discover a connection between the absurd situations and supernatural occurrences. As Connor's adventures unfold, Cassie's parallel subplot delves deeper into the mysterious forces at play, ultimately converging with the main plot.

Name: Richard "Richie" Thompson

Age: 40

Job: Stand-up comedian

Role: Unknown enemy

Appearance: Charismatic, well-dressed, always with a mischievous smile

Personality: Manipulative, cunning, deceptive

Background

Richie is a successful stand-up comedian who seems to have a personal vendetta against Connor. He uses his wit and charm to manipulate others and sabotage Connor's life, creating further chaos and absurdity.

Name: Olivia Sullivan

    Age: 32

    Job: Yoga instructor

    Role: Friend turned foe

    Appearance: Graceful, physically fit, always calm and composed

    Personality: Zen, nurturing, secretly vengeful

    Background

Olivia is Connor's close friend who appears to be a calming influence in his life. However, as the story progresses, it is revealed that Olivia has a hidden agenda and seeks revenge on Connor for a past transgression, turning their friendship into a dangerous game of cat and mouse.

Name: Henry Johnson

Age: 60

Job: Retired magician

Role: Mentor

Appearance: Wearing a top hat, a long cape, and carrying a magic wand

Personality: Enigmatic, mischievous, wise

Background

Henry is a retired magician who becomes an unexpected mentor to Connor. With his vast knowledge of illusions and tricks, he helps Connor navigate through the absurd situations, teaching him how to embrace the unexpected and find humor in the chaos.

More titles by the same author:
ROMANCE
Crossed Destinies
Love In Paris
Love Tastes Like The Sea
Romance On The Island
Taste Of Passion
MYSTERY/SUSPENSE
Amnesia
Blood In The Mansion
Cursed Forest
Deadly Enigma
Deadly Game
Deadly Secrets
Dirty Business
Killer On Board
Lethal Therapy
Macabre Game
Missing
Museum Robbery
Riddles
COMEDY
An Ordinary Man
CHILDREN'S STORIES
Bedtime Stories To Read

About the Author

This author was born on February 18, 1969, in Montevideo, Uruguay. He pursued his studies at the University ORT. He possesses a highly active and fertile imagination, along with a persistent interest in learning and expanding his mental horizons. He enjoys traveling, engaging in philosophical discussions, and exchanging ideas with individuals from diverse backgrounds and perspectives. As an independent and free thinker, he is a progressive, open-minded individual who embraces new technologies, scientific advancements, and the latest discoveries in any field. His mind operates intuitively and non-linearly, often experiencing sudden flashes of inspiration seemingly out of nowhere. With a gentle and poetic soul, he holds a deep love and affinity for music. He views music as a natural language, as many of his emotions are nebulous and elusive, making it challenging to verbalize his experiences of life. Furthermore, he is profoundly romantic and frequently finds himself 'in love with love.'" Passionate explorer of emotions, as a novelist, he has taken readers on fearless journeys through unsolved mysteries, high-voltage suspense, and fiery romances. Each page is a world to be discovered, where secrets lurk in every shadow and hearts intertwine in a passionate dance. His words are like magnets, drawing readers into a world where suspense intertwines with romance, and passion burns as brightly as intrigue. Each work is an invitation to immerse oneself in a whirlwind of emotions, where unexpected twists keep readers on the edge of their seats, and sighs of love make them daydream. If you're looking for a read that transports you to enigmatic worlds, makes your heart race with every page turn, and makes you sigh with every love story, then I invite you to delve into his captivating novels of mystery, suspense, and romance. Get ready for an unforgettable literary experience, where mystery and love intertwine in a passionate embrace.

Read more at https://www.alvarofigares.com.